Teatime in Space

First published in the UK in 2008 by
QED Publishing
A Quarto Group company
226 City Road
London EC1V 2TT
www.qed-publishing.co.uk

A catalogue record for this book is available
from the British Library.

ISBN 978 1 84538 957 4

Author Caroline Castle
Illustrator Paul Nicholls
Editor Clare Weaver
Designer Alix Wood
Consultant Anne Faundez

Publisher Steve Evans
Creative Director Zeta Davies

Printed and bound in China

Teatime in Space

Caroline Castle

Illustrated by
Paul Nicholls

QED Publishing

QED

One afternoon, a spaceship landed in Pete's back garden in a shower of sparks.

"Wow!"
said Pete.

A small, green creature climbed down.

"Greetings, pink one," said the creature. "I am Zub of Planet Flub."

"Greetings, green one," said Pete. "I am Pete of Planet Earth."

"Can you help me?" said Zub. "My Flubmobile has broken down. Mumbo of Zub will be very cross if I am late for tea."

Pete examined the little spaceship.
Zub showed him the controls.

Pete saw the problem at once.
The down button was stuck.
He **wiggled** it and he **waggled** it.

But then...

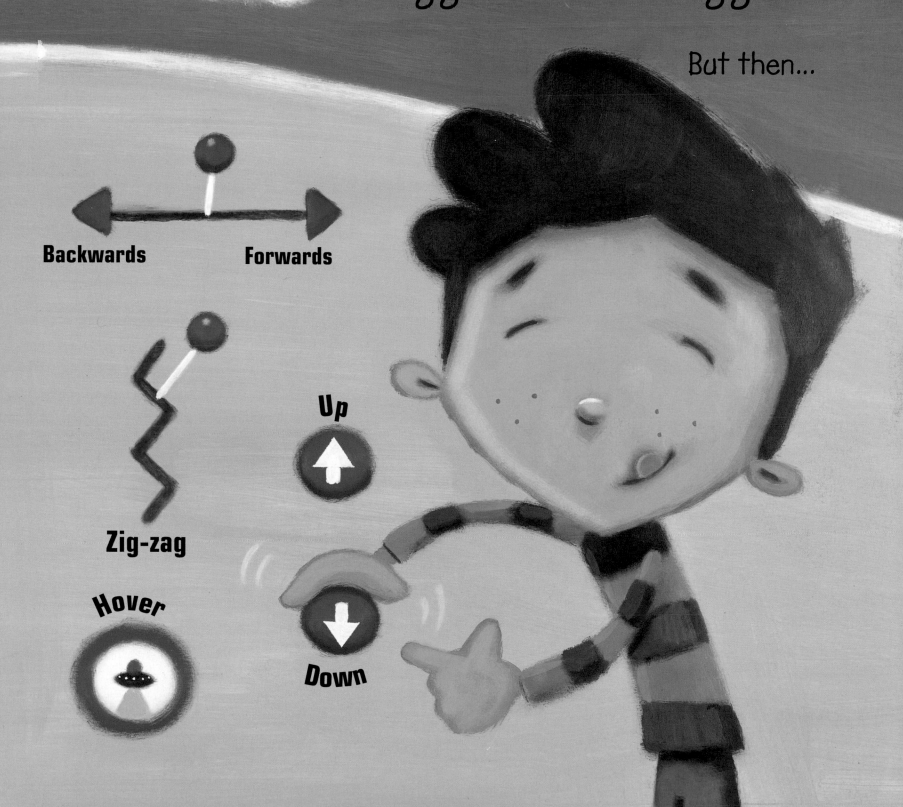

The little spaceship took off.

Zoom

All of a sudden, they were in outer space!

"Oh, no!" cried Pete.
"Quick, let's push the down button again!"

Pete and Zub pushed the button
as hard as they could.
But the spaceship
just zoomed higher and
higher and higher.

"Oh, no!" cried Pete. "Mumbo of Pete will be very cross.
It's my teatime soon, and I'm not allowed to go beyond the
garden gate. Let alone into **outer space!**"

"Sorry," said Zub.
"But it's on autopilot.
Any minute now, we will be on Planet Flub."

At that very moment,

the little spaceship landed - bump! - on Planet Flub.

Mumbo of Zub came rushing from the house.
She was not pleased.

"Naughty Zub!" she cried. "You know you are
not allowed to go beyond the garden stars.
And who is this strange pink creature?"

Zub told Mumbo all about his adventure on Planet Earth, and how Pete had helped him to mend the little spaceship.

Mumbo of Zub was so grateful to Pete, she invited him to tea.

Pete looked at his watch. Mumbo of Pete would be calling him in ten minutes. There was just enough time.

Then Pete said he really must go.

Pete said goodbye to Flub,
then Mumbo of Zub
flew him home – zap!
– in her Superzoom Zippership.

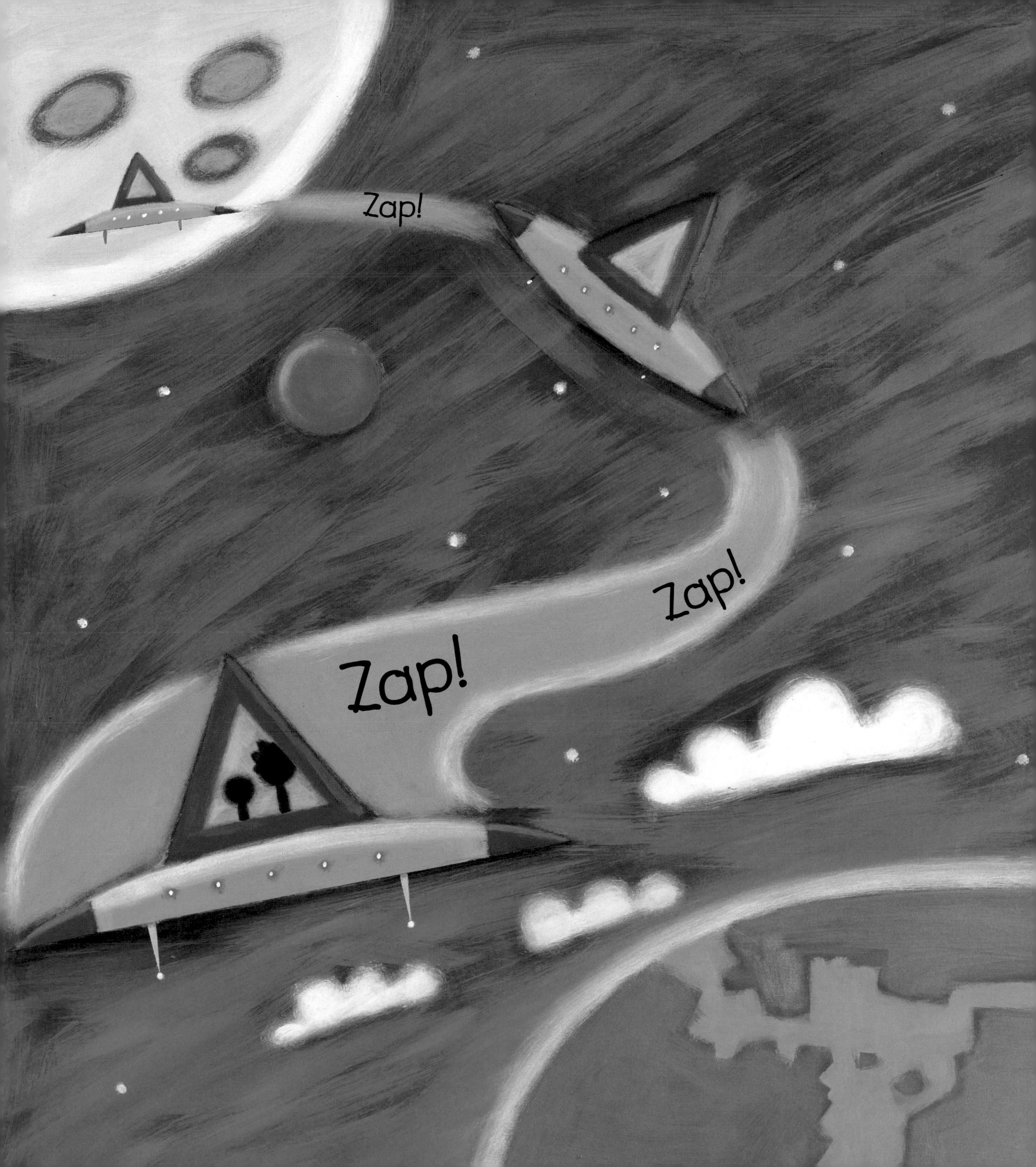
Zap!
Zap!
Zap!

He arrived just in time for tea on Planet Earth.

It was fish fingers on brown toast with a glass of fizzy orange.

Pete wasn't the least bit hungry.

But he ate it
all up anyway.

After all, he could hardly tell Mum
that he had already had his tea...

– in **space!**

Notes for teachers and parents

- Look at the front cover of the book together. Talk about the picture. Can the children guess what the story is going to be about? Read the title together.

- When the children first read the story (or had it read to them), how did they think the story was going to end? Were they right? Discuss other ideas of how the story might have ended.

- Ask the children to take it in turns to try to read the story aloud. Help them with any difficult words and remember to praise the children for their efforts in reading the book.

- Explain that the Earth is a planet, too. Can the children name any other planets? Look at a picture of the solar system and ask the children if they can find Earth. Point out and name the other major planets. Zub's Planet Flub is too small to feature on the picture! Ask the children to choose a location for Planet Flub (not too far away from Earth!).

- Is there life in space? Many people think they have seen flying saucers, but it has never been proved so we just don't know! Encourage the children to invent their own space creatures – what might they look like, and what would they be called? Get them to draw pictures of their creatures and design a spaceship of their own.

- In pairs, the children can take on the roles of Pete and Flub, and act out the dialogue throughout the book.

- Although Pete and Flub come from different planets, they both have families who do the same things! Discuss with the children why both Pete and Flub are not allowed beyond the garden gate/garden stars on their own. For example, they might get lost (which is exactly what happened to Flub!), or have an accident.

- Pete and Flub eat very different food! Discuss what types of different food children eat in other parts of the world. What might children have for tea in India or China, for instance?

- Ask the children, with a parent, to look at the night sky just before bedtime. Explain that they may be able to see the stars and the Moon. Discuss with them the fact that humans have landed on the Moon, and perhaps one day life will be found in space.